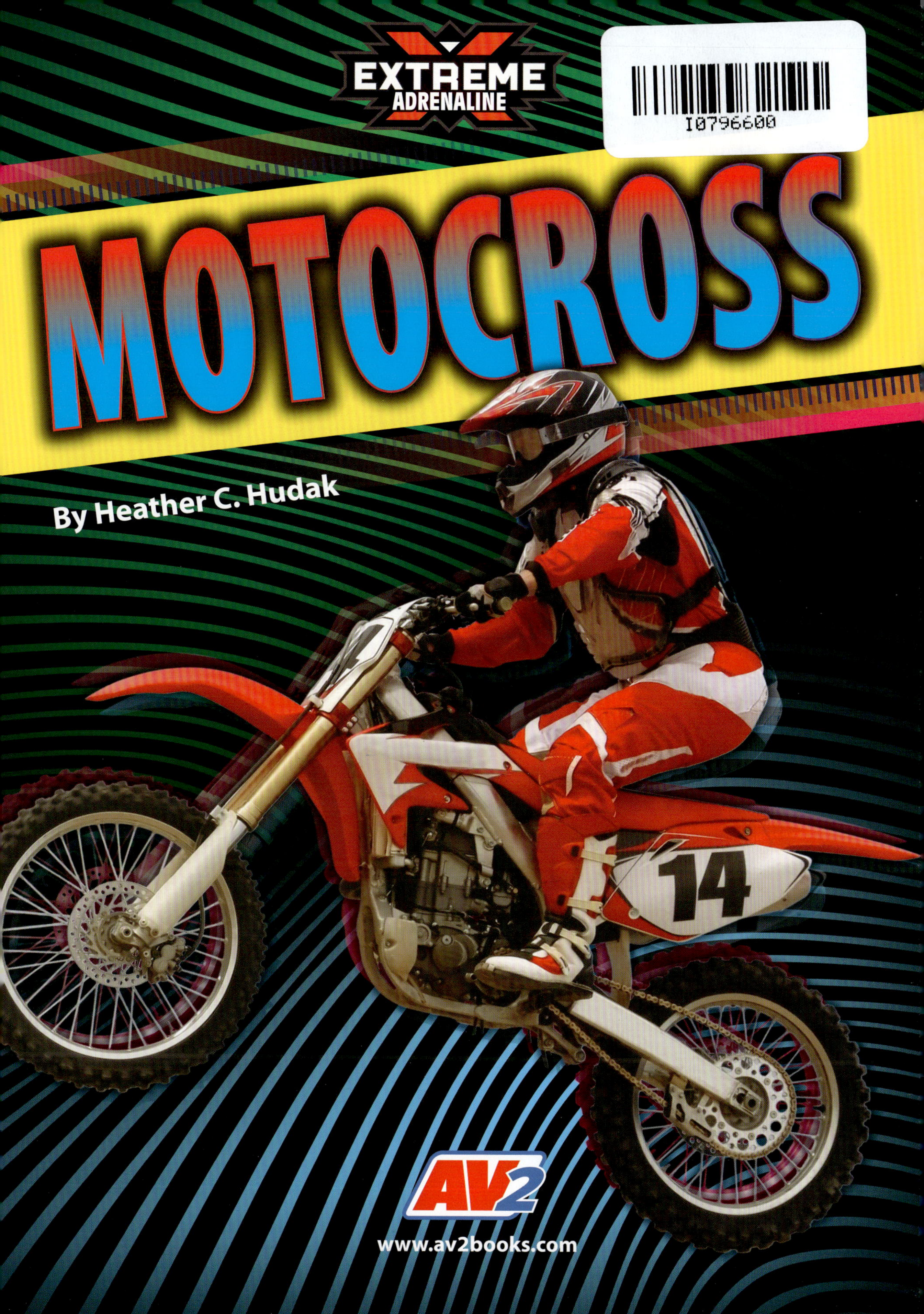
EXTREME
ADRENALINE
MOTOCROSS
By Heather C. Hudak
14
AV2
www.av2books.com

Step 1
Go to **www.av2books.com**

Step 2
Enter this unique code
FXBUMHES3

Step 3
Explore your interactive eBook!

AV2 is optimized for use on any device

Your interactive eBook comes with...

Contents
Browse a live contents page to easily navigate through resources

Audio
Listen to sections of the book read aloud

Videos
Watch informative video clips

Weblinks
Gain additional information for research

Try This!
Complete activities and hands-on experiments

Key Words
Study vocabulary, and complete a matching word activity

Quizzes
Test your knowledge

Slideshows
View images and captions

... and much, much more!

MOTOCROSS

WHAT ARE THE X GAMES?

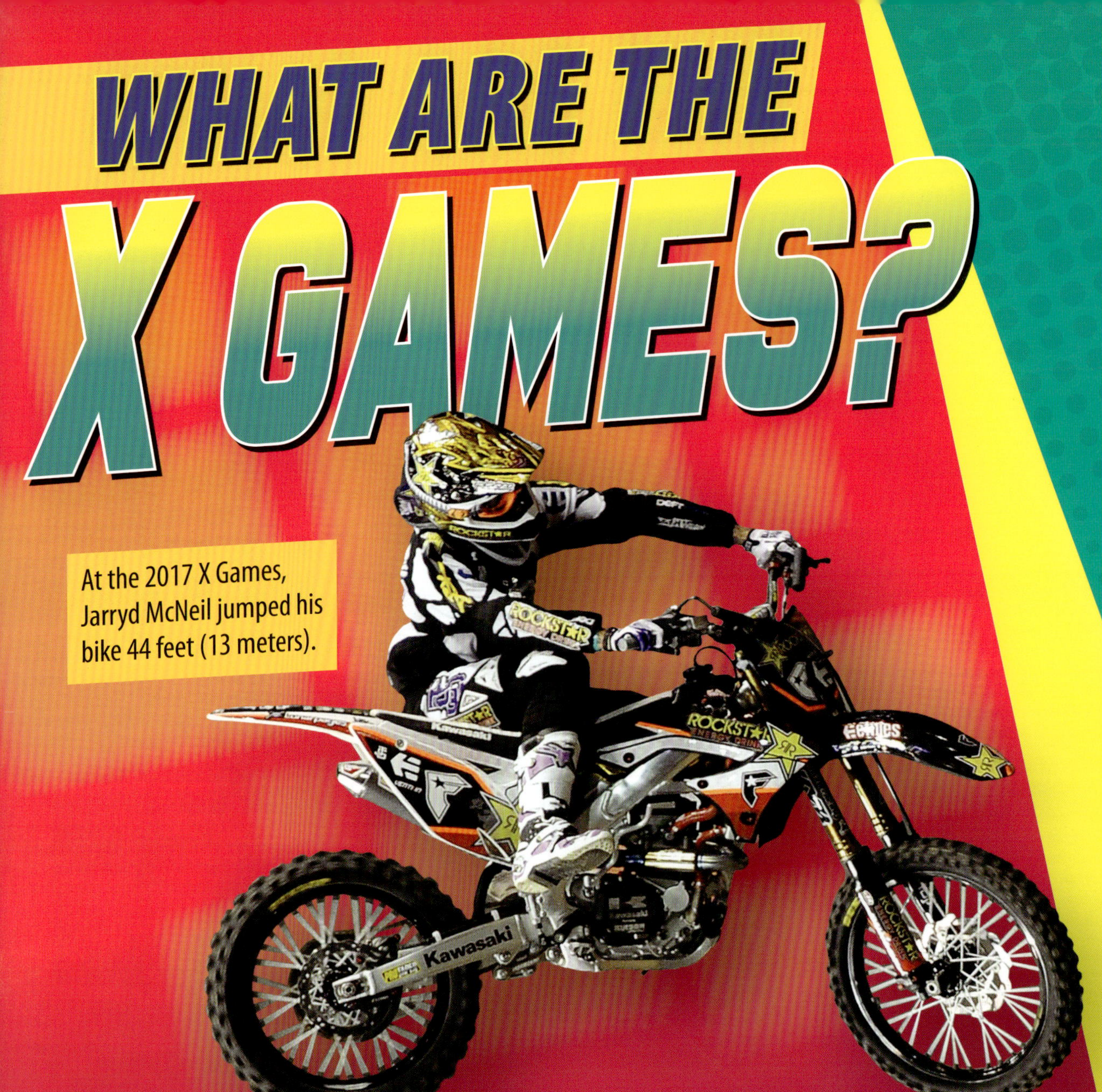

At the 2017 X Games, Jarryd McNeil jumped his bike 44 feet (13 meters).

The X Games are a series of sports events for the best in extreme sports.

Extreme sports are done at high speeds. **Athletes** must wear special gear to help keep them safe. Events such as the X Games show off the skill and hard work of the athletes. These events also show how difficult extreme sports are.

Some of the best motocross, or moto X, riders in the world come to the X Games. These riders show off extreme moves. X Games events have riders doing stunts in the air or racing to the finish line.

X FEST

The X Games have more than just sports. Each year, bands from all over the world play for fans at the X Games. X Fest is the name of the X Games concert. There is punk rock, hip-hop, and alternative music. The bands perform between events. They keep the crowds excited for the games.

X Fest 2019 was held at the Armory in Minneapolis, Minnesota, which can host up to 8,400 people.

Speed Demons

Motocross riders can reach 85 miles (137 kilometers) per hour.

Wear and Tear

Motocross tires often need to be replaced after only 100 hours of use.

Mixing It Up

X Games riders usually have three to five bikes.

WHAT IS MOTOCROSS?

Motocross is an intense sport. It is difficult and dangerous. Riders need skill, balance, and determination.

In this sport, athletes ride on special motorcycles. These advanced machines are lightweight. They race over obstacles and **off-road** tracks. Some riders perform flips and tricks in freestyle motocross.

At the X Games, there are several freestyle events. They include Best Whip, Step Up, and Freestyle. During these events, riders show off a variety of skills. They earn points from judges and excite the fans.

MOTOCROSS TIMELINE

1885 Gottlieb Daimler designs a motorized bicycle that has wooden wheels and a combustion engine.

1959 The first motocross races are held in the United States.

1972 The first stadium motocross event is held at the Los Angeles Coliseum.

1991 Jose Yanez is the first person to ever attempt a **backflip** off a motocross bike.

1998 Moto X starts as a demonstration sport at the X Games.

2006 Travis Pastrana lands the first-ever double backflip in the X Games Best Trick final event.

2015 The X Games hold the first-ever Moto X QuarterPipe event. Thomas Pages wins after landing a bike flip.

2019 Jarryd McNeil makes history as the first motocross rider to win gold medals four years in a row in the same discipline at the X Games.

ALL THE RIGHT EQUIPMENT

To protect against falls, motocross riders wear suits. They are made up of jerseys and pants. The long-sleeve jerseys fit over protective gear. The pants are long and padded.

A chest protector is made of hard plastic. It acts as a shield across the rider's front.

Knee and elbow guards are also hard plastic covers. They strap to the joints. The guards help prevent major injuries.

Longest Jump

The longest jump landed on a motocross bike was 322 feet (98 m).

Weighing In

A motocross bike weighs about 215 pounds (97.5 kilograms).

Illegal Rides

It is illegal to ride motocross bikes on public streets and highways.

Helmet

The helmet is the most important piece of safety equipment. Helmets have saved many riders from serious head injuries.

Goggles and Gloves

All motocross riders must wear goggles and gloves. These protect their eyes and hands.

Suspension

Motocross bikes have plenty of **suspension**. Riders can tackle large jumps and rough courses.

Seat

The long, flat seat allows riders to shift their weight quickly, which provides more **traction** in corners.

Bikes

Most motocross bikes are smaller than traditional motorcycles.

WHERE TO RIDE

Motocross parks include low ridges that riders can push off when taking corners.

Freestyle motocross can be done in large open spaces with plenty of dirt. Natural tracks can be found on public land. Often they have ramps, hills, and jumps made of rock and dirt. Some riders build homemade tracks. They can have ramps of all different heights and lengths.

Before events, riders take practice runs to get familiar with the track.

Specially made tracks are found at the X Games. They are built for safety. They also let riders reach maximum height for their extreme tricks.

Riders launch from wooden ramps. At the bottom is a landing area with a dirt ramp. It slows down riders. In some cases, there may be a **deceleration** ramp as well. Most often, these ramps have foam bumpers on the sides for safety.

BEST WHIP

Josh Sheehan has claimed 11 X Games medals, including bronze at X Games Shanghai 2019.

One of the newest events in X Games Moto X is called Best Whip. It started in 2013. Best Whip replaced a similar event called Best Trick. Both test a rider's ability to do daring stunts in midair while on their bike.

Riders do not do vertical rotations in Best Whip. Those include somersaults and backflips. Instead, they earn points based on style. The amount of time spent in the air is measured. How much they rotate their bikes horizontally is also judged.

Jarryd McNeil has nine X Games gold medals. Five are for Best Whip.

When the event starts, the riders have six minutes. They take laps around the track. Then they launch off the big ramp. Riders shoot into the air. They perform tricks for the audience.

Fans then vote for their favorites. They can use the internet and social media to cast votes.

Best Whip Past Winners

X Games Minneapolis 2019

Gold – Tyler Bereman
Silver – Tom Parsons
Bronze – Jarryd McNeil

X Games Minneapolis 2018

Gold – Jarryd McNeil
Silver – Genki Watanabe
Bronze – Axell Hodges

STEP UP

As of 2019, Massimo Bianconcini had claimed one silver and two bronze medals in the Step Up event.

Step Up is a high jump moto X event. It has been in the X Games since 2000. Step Up uses a steeper ramp than Best Whip. Workers spend hours to make the dirt ramp. It towers almost 30 feet (9.1 m) high.

Two vertical bars are placed on either side of the ramp. A horizontal bar is laid on top of them. The bar is 26 feet (8 m) above the top of the ramp.

Jarryd McNeil cleared 43 feet (13 m) to take Step Up gold at the 2018 X Games.

Five riders take turns. First, they ride up the ramp. Then, they try to jump over the horizontal bar. All riders get two tries. If they cannot do it, they are eliminated. Once each rider has tried the jump, the bar is raised. It goes up 6 inches (15 centimeters). The contest starts again. This goes on until only one rider remains.

Step Up Past Winners

X Games Minneapolis 2019

Gold – Jarryd McNeil
Silver – Bryce Hudson
Bronze – Colby Raha, Ronnie Renner (tie)

X Games Minneapolis 2018

Gold – Jarryd McNeil
Silver – Libor Podmol
Bronze – Colby Raha

FREESTYLE

Taka Higashino has three gold medals in X Games Freestyle.

Since 1999, the Freestyle has been an important event in the X Games. Travis Pastrana won the first event. He also set a record with 99.00 points out of 100.

In Freestyle, riders can perform two routines. If they do well the first time, they often skip the second run. The course includes dirt mounds. Each has a different height and angles. Sometimes there are small quarterpipes or ramps. Riders can choose the jumps and the tricks they perform.

Rob Adelberg's first run scored 87.00. His second run earned him the gold, with a score of 92.33.

Judges observe each routine. They award points based on the variety of tricks. Points are also given for difficult stunts. The Freestyle format encourages riders to try new moves to impress the judges. It also allows athletes to be creative. They can express their unique styles.

Freestyle Past Winners

X Games Minneapolis 2019

Gold – Rob Adelberg
Silver – Josh Sheehan
Bronze – Jackson Strong

X Games Minneapolis 2018

Gold – Tom Pages
Silver – Jackson Strong
Bronze – Rob Adelberg

TURNING PRO

Monster Energy sponsors many motocross athletes, including Ben Watson.

The first step to becoming a pro motocross rider is to get sponsored. Companies pick exciting riders to sponsor. They give the athletes money. It can be used for equipment, travel, and living expenses. Riders will wear the company's name or **logo** at events.

At each X Games, only the gold medalists from the last year are guaranteed a spot. A committee chooses the other riders. The committee selects athletes based on three **criteria**.

Vicki Golden is one of the few professional female motocross athletes.

First, the committee looks at the results from all major freestyle motocross events. Riders with top scores are more likely to be invited back.

Second, the committee looks at popularity and **media** coverage. Athletes with larger fan bases are more likely to be chosen. Third, riders who show exceptional skill are given an invitation.

Once a rider is chosen, there is still work to do. Riders train constantly, using private tracks. They often hire trainers. If a rider is not chosen for the next X Games, he or she continues to train. Riders work hard to improve their skills.

OTHER EXTREME SPORTS

Motocross is a unique sport. It is popular around the world. It is not the only sport with motorcycles or bikes. These sports are similar to motocross.

BMX

In BMX, or Bicycle Motocross, athletes use special bicycles. They race or perform stunts. BMX can be done on almost any type of surface. This includes dirt or concrete. Many freestyle BMX riders use rails, ramps, jumps, and other obstacles to perform tricks. BMX racers speed along dirt tracks. The first rider to reach the finish line wins.

ATVs

ATVs, or all-terrain vehicles, are meant for off-road trails. They are also used for racing and multi-terrain events. ATVs can handle dirt, sand, and other natural obstacles.

Mountain Biking

In mountain biking, people ride special bikes over rocky trails. These bikes have wide tires that grip the ground better than thin tires.

Auto Racing

In some types of auto races, cars complete a set number of laps around a track. In others, cars race toward a finish line. The first car to reach this mark wins the race.

UNFORGETTABLE MOMENTS

During the X Games, there have been many unforgettable moments. Some of these are record-breaking wins, long falls, and new tricks.

At the X Games in 2003, Brian Deegan was competing. Deegan had won gold in Best Trick the year before. He wanted to impress the judges again. Deegan pulled off a new trick. It was a 360-degree rotation in the air, with a perfect landing. Deegan took home Best Trick gold, as well as the bronze in Freestyle.

Mike Metzger made history at the 2002 X Games. From a 10-foot (3-m) ramp, he did a backflip. From the next ramp, he landed a second backflip. This was the first time a rider landed two backflips in a row.

In 2019, moto X events made their debut in Norway during the 2019 X Games. Best Trick, Best Whip, and QuarterPipe High Air were featured. Corey Creed set a new record height for QuarterPipe. Creed reached 40.65 feet (12.39 m). This run earned him the gold.

MOTOCROSS AROUND THE WORLD

Motocross riders travel all over the globe to visit motocross parks. Use this map and research online to discover your next motocross park. Then, answer the questions to test your knowledge.

Durhamtown Plantation
Georgia, United States

- Has 150 miles (241 km) of trails
- Among the largest off-road resorts in the United States

Circuit El Terre
Almenar, Cataluña, Spain

- One track, about a mile (1.5 km) in length
- Course is extremely difficult, with 11 banks to the right and 8 to the left

Fat Cats Motoparc
South Yorkshire, England

- Has three tracks
- On-site hotel so riders can stay overnight and ride multiple days

QMP Moto Park Coulson
Queensland, Australia

- Only facility in Australia to receive government funding
- Several tracks that are only for children

TEST YOUR KNOWLEDGE

1. Which country has the most motocross parks?
2. Which U.S. cities have hosted the Summer X Games in the last three years?

X GAMES VENUES

= Summer X Games Host City

1. Newport, Rhode Island, USA
2. San Diego, California, USA
3. San Francisco, California, USA
4. Los Angeles, California, USA
5. Austin, Texas, USA
6. Minneapolis, Minnesota, USA
7. Boise, Idaho, USA
8. Mexico City, Mexico
9. Foz do Iguaçu, Brazil
10. Kuala Lumpur, Malaysia
11. Shanghai, China
12. Seoul, South Korea
13. Phuket, Thailand
14. Barcelona, Spain
15. Munich, Germany
16. Sydney, Australia

MODERN STARS

TYLER BEREMAN

Hometown
Templeton, California, United States

Born
August 27, 1991

NOTES

- Started motocross racing at 10 years old
- Six-time X Games medalist, with one gold, two silvers, and five bronze medals

VICKI GOLDEN

Hometown
San Diego, California, United States

Born
July 28, 1992

NOTES

- Began her motocross racing career at age 7
- Came in sixth for Best Whip at the 2016 X Games and eighth in 2019

RONNIE RENNER

Hometown
Leesburg, Florida, United States

Born
June 10, 1977

NOTES

- Set the world record in Step Up in 2007, hitting a vertical distance of 35 feet, 6 inches (10.8 m)
- Took bronze in Step Up at the X Games in 2019
- Runs his own training facility

JARRYD MCNEIL

Hometown
Yarrawonga, Australia

Born
July 20, 1991

NOTES

- Started riding dirt bikes before the age of 3
- First moto X rider to win four consecutive gold medals in a single discipline
- Most Best Whip medals, with nine

MOTOCROSS LEGENDS

Hometown
Tallahassee, Florida, United States

Born
November 27, 1979

NOTES
- Known as the GOAT, or the Greatest of All Time
- Holds the most records of any moto X rider

Hometown
Seal Beach, California, United States

Born
July 17, 1975

NOTES
- Became a professional motocross rider at the age of 17
- Signature trick is the "Hart Attack," a mid-air handstand

CHUCK CAROTHERS

Hometown
Hattiesburg, Mississippi, United States

Born
June 20, 1978

NOTES
- Won gold in Best Trick at X Games 2004 when he landed a "**Carolla**"
- Has had 21 broken bones and 13 surgeries

JEREMY STENBERG

Hometown
San Diego, California, United States

Born
September 27, 1981

NOTES
- Started riding at the age of 2
- Has won six gold, five silver, and five bronze X Games medals

QUIZ

1 Motocross riders can reach speeds of how many miles per hour?

2 After how many hours of use do motocross tires need to be replaced?

3 In what year did moto X start as a demonstration sport at the X Games?

4 Are motocross bikes smaller or larger than traditional motorcycles?

5 Which event did Best Whip replace in 2013?

6 How many inches is the bar raised in Step Up after each stage?

7 In Freestyle, how many routines can riders perform?

8 How did Mike Metzger make history in 2002?

9 Where is one of America's largest off-road resorts located?

10 Which motocross star began a racing career at age 7?

Answers

1. 85 (137 km)
2. 100
3. 1998
4. Smaller
5. Best Trick
6. 6 (15 cm)
7. Two
8. He landed two backflips in a row.
9. Georgia
10. Vicki Golden

KEY WORDS

athletes: people who train for and take part in sporting events

backflip: a trick done when the rider does a backwards somersault in the air

Carolla: a trick in which the rider reaches a height of 25 feet (7.6 m) in the air, lets go of the bike, and spins the body 360 degrees while laying above the bike

criteria: a list of items used to make a judgment or decision

deceleration: the act or process of slowing down

logo: the symbol or image a company uses to represent itself

media: television, radio, internet, and other forms of mass communication

off-road: a sport where specially designed vehicles are driven on rugged terrain, away from main roads or trails

suspension: the arrangement of springs, or shock absorbers

traction: the grip of a tire on a surface

INDEX

Get the best of both worlds.

AV2 bridges the gap between print and digital.

The expandable resources toolbar enables quick access to content including **videos**, **audio**, **activities**, **weblinks**, **slideshows**, **quizzes**, and **key words**.

Animated videos make static images come alive.

Resource icons on each page help readers to further **explore key concepts**.

Published by AV2
350 5th Avenue, 59th Floor
New York, NY 10118
Website: www.av2books.com

Library of Congress Control Number: 2019047762

ISBN 978-1-7911-1832-7 (hardcover)
ISBN 978-1-7911-1833-4 (softcover)
ISBN 978-1-7911-1834-1 (multi-user eBook)
ISBN 978-1-7911-1835-8 (single user eBook)

Printed in Guangzhou, China
1 2 3 4 5 6 7 8 9 0 24 23 22 21 20

032020
101319

Project Coordinator: Ryan Smith
Designer: Terry Paulhus

AV2 acknowledges Getty Images, iStock, Newscom, Wikimedia, and Shutterstock as its primary image suppliers for this title.